F

For Michaela, Rosemary and Sophy
and for Timothy

Scholastic Book Services Inc.,
10 Earlham Street, London, WC2H 9LN, England

Scholastic Book Services Inc.,
730 Broadway, New York N.Y. 10003, U.S.A.

Scholastic Tab Publications Ltd.,
123 Newkirk Road, Richmond Hill, Ontario L4C 3G5, Canada

Ashton Scholastic Pty Ltd., PO Box 579,
Gosford, New South Wales, Australia

Ashton Scholastic Ltd.,
165 Marua Road, Panmure, Auckland, New Zealand

First published 1982 by Blackie and Son Ltd.

Published in paperback by Scholastic Book Services, Inc. 1984
Text copyright © Janice Elliott 1982
Illustrations copyright ©Philippe Dupasquier 1982

THE INCOMPETENT DRAGON

Janice Elliott

Illustrated by Philippe Dupasquier

Hippo Books
Scholastic Book Services
London

Christopher Magnifico did not like to stay with his Aunt Pen. She lived in a black house and had a nose like a knife. Christopher had to stay with her quite often because his mother was a dancer and his father was an acrobat. They loved him dearly, but because they were so busy dancing and flying through the air with the greatest of ease, they could never take him on holiday.

'One day when our ship comes in we will take you on holiday,' said Mr Magnifico as he went off to work. Mrs Magnifico took Christopher to his Aunt's. When she left she hugged him very tight.

'Goodbye, my sweet pudding-pie,' she said, mopped up a big shining tear and, before she could cry, danced away down the street.

Aunt Pen's black house was on a black cliff by a grey sea. She had no flowers in her garden, only concrete, so that the children should not pick the flowers. She had no friends, only a fierce cat. The cat was black and his name was Black Cat. While Christopher Magnifico and Aunt Pen ate dry bread and semolina, Black Cat ate fat silver fish, jellies, peanut-butter sandwiches, chips, steak-and-kidney pie and ice cream. When Christopher Magnifico arrived Aunt Pen said, as she always did: 'I don't know what I shall do with you. I do not know about boys. You had better go to bed.'

So Christopher went to bed too early. His room was mostly grey with a black blind and a grey bedspread. He thought of his mother dancing and his father flying through the air with the greatest of ease, and he felt very sad. He would much rather not have had a holiday at all than come to the black house on the black cliff. He closed his eyes tight shut so that he would not shed a tear. He listened to the wind from the west howling against the window-pane and growling in the chimney.

Crash! Whoomph! Thump!

Christopher, who had been dreaming that his ship had come in, sat up and rubbed his eyes.

There was a kind of a glow by the hearth and a dreadful pile of soot. Sitting on the pile of soot looking very dusty and rather cross was a *crocodile.*

'Dear me,' said the crocodile, 'another crash landing. I do *wish* people would sweep their chimneys. I don't suppose, by chance, you would have a cucumber sandwich and a nice cup of tea?'

'Excuse me,' said Christopher. 'I didn't know that crocodiles ate cucumber sandwiches.'

'CROCODILES!' cried the beast, who was now licking his scales with an air of distaste. 'HOW could you IMAGINE that I am a CROCODILE? Nasty wet snappy pointless things, with very bad manners. Here I am come at great effort and my own expense to bring you a bit of magic and instead of cucumber sandwiches I get rude remarks. I am a DRAGON, boy, DRAGON! As in St George and the dragon. Mythical monster sometimes fire breathing.'

'What's mythical?' asked Christopher.

'A myth is something that is true if you believe in it.' The dragon was looking more cheerful now. 'Well,' he said, 'if there are to be no cucumber sandwiches we may as well go to sleep.'

Christopher knew he should let the dragon go to sleep, but there was just one question he had to ask.

'Dragon?'

'Yes? Yes, Yes?' said the dragon, pretending to wake up, 'what is it now? Some helpless soul requiring an emergency spell? Witches? Warlocks? Weasels? Measles? No wonder it's three million years since I had a holiday.'

'Well, Dragon, all I wondered was, why did you come to do magic for me? I mean how did it happen that I needed magic, and then there you were?'

'To tell you the truth, dear boy, it was stress of weather–port in any storm. There I was, flying along, when up comes storm force ten. Soaked to the scales I am, and not licensed, you see, to fly in gales. So down your chimney I popped, and here I am.'

Christopher thought the dragon was a bit of a show-off but he liked him. *Much* better than crocodiles.

In the morning Christopher and Aunt Pen had porridge for breakfast. Black Cat had four fried eggs, and bacon and mushrooms *and* fried bread, toast with marmalade, two kippers and a bowl of cream.

While Black Cat cleaned his whiskers, Aunt Pen said, 'I am going to buy some nice salmon for Black Cat's lunch. I do not know about boys. You will have to look after yourself. If you paddle you must not get your feet wet.'

The moment Aunt Pen had gone out there was a slithering, scratching noise on the stairs. Black Cat leaped on top of the highest cupboard and stood there hissing and spitting.

There, at the bottom of the stairs, sat the dragon, shaking all over with his head under his wing.

'Hello Dragon,' said Christopher. 'Aren't you feeling well?'

'Actually,' said the dragon, 'I am terrified of cats. Absolutely *terrified*.' He looked embarrassed. 'The truth is, I'm not much of a success as a dragon. I can't even breathe fire.'

'Poor Dragon,' said Christopher. 'I think you're very nice. We can go for a paddle, if you like, if we don't get our feet wet.'

Walking down to the beach, Christopher was surprised that people were not surprised to see a dragon.

'Well, well, that's a big lizard,' said the lady in the sweet shop.

'Funny dog you've got there,' said the postman.

'People see what they expect to see,' said the dragon, who was looking more cheerful now.

They played with a ball, built a sandcastle (the dragon was very good at digging), then sat on a rock in the sun. And the dragon said:

'Well then, what about a spot of magic? Shall we turn Aunt Pen into a frog or Black Cat into a dog?'

Christopher was usually a very nice boy, but suddenly he felt *mean*.

So it was that Aunt Pen turned into a frog and Black Cat into a dog. But as the dragon was not very good at magic, Black Cat still said Miaow.

'Miaow,' said Black Cat, who was now Black Dog, and chased Aunt Frog round the room.

Black Dog went out into the concrete garden to bark. 'Miaow,' said Black Dog, and all the dogs laughed at him until they nearly burst, while the birds fell off the branches laughing.

Christopher and the dragon had a good day of magic. They flew over land and sea to the dawn of the world, but there was a headwind coming back and they landed at the North Pole for a minute by mistake.

They had a lovely supper at the North Pole, even if the dragon did get his spells mixed up. They had sardines on crumpets and jam on sausages and hamburgers with treacle.

'Dear me,' sighed the dragon. 'What I wouldn't give for a plain straightforward cucumber sandwich. Well, I suppose it is time we got you home to bed.'

'That was a *lovely* day,' yawned Christopher. 'Thank you, Dragon.'

When he got back to the house on the cliff and saw Black Dog miaowing and found Aunt Frog hiding piteously in the drain, Christopher didn't feel mean any more.

After thinking very hard with his head in his claws, the dragon turned Black Dog back into Black Cat and Aunt Frog back into Aunt Pen. But either there had been a muddle in his magic, or they had learned their lessons, because Black Cat was now a very nice, purry cat, not greedy at all, and Aunt Pen was very jolly.

'Well!' laughed Aunt Pen, 'whatever am I doing in the drain?' She hugged Christopher and was very polite to the dragon. 'But oh!' she cried, 'how I wish I did not have a black house and a concrete garden!'

Christopher winked at the dragon. At once by magic the

house was redecorated entirely from top to bottom in lovely cheerful colours. As for the garden, the dragon made almost his best spell ever: in place of the concrete there were daffodils and hollyhocks, Michaelmas daisies, roses, forget-me-nots, bluebells and lilies – all the flowers of every season blooming at the same time. There were even some flowers no one had ever heard of or seen before, like blue sunflowers and pink narcissi. They were really a mistake of the dragon's magic, but he pretended he had invented them. Aunt Pen clapped her hands and hugged the dragon, not minding his scales at all.

Finally the dragon made his last and best spell of all. A beautiful little steam-boat, very trim and cheerful, came steaming in from the sea. On the deck were waving Mr and Mrs Magnifico.

'Our ship's come in at last!' cried Mr Magnifico. 'Now we can take you on holiday!'

'Oh, my sweet pudding-pie,' sang out Mrs Magnifico, dancing up the quay to hug Christopher very tight.

The dragon said he would have to get back. First though, they had a lovely party in Aunt Pen's pretty house. There were hot-dogs and haggis, buns and blancmanges, treacle and trifle, cake and crackers. The dragon even agreed to sit next to Black Cat, who was very polite and passed him cucumber sandwiches.

As cats go, he's quite a good fellow,' whispered the dragon to Christopher, and no one told him not to whisper at the table.

'And now, dear boy I fear I must be off.'

Christopher felt sad that his friend would be leaving.

'Where will you go, Dragon?'

'Well,' said the dragon, 'I should go back to my hoard. But ever since St George gave us a bad name it's not been the same for dragons. Magic's not what it was, either. So I think I might retire to the dawn of the world and put up my claws.'

So when they had finished the party everyone went outside to wave goodbye. The dragon's take-off was rather bumpy but at last he was up and away, looking very splendid against the sunset.

'Goodbye, Dragon,' called Christopher, then they all went to bed because magic is tiring. Afterwards they went right round the world in the little steam-boat, eating ice cream.

Christopher Magnifico never forgot the day his boat came in. And all his life he believed in dragons, so that they would be true.